# THE OGRE OF THREEPEAKS

## A NOVELLA OF QORUNN

### STEFON MEARS

Thousand
Faces
Publishing

# Also by Stefon Mears

**The Rise of Magic Series**
*Magician's Choice*
*Sleight of Mind*
*Lunar Alchemy*
*Three Fae Monte*
*The Sphinx Principle*
*Double Backed Magic*
*Mercury Fold (coming soon)*

**Cavan Oltblood Series**
*Half a Wizard*
*The Ice Dagger*
*Spells of Undeath*

**Power City Tales**
*Not Quite Bulletproof*
*No Money in Heroism*

**Standalones**
*Between the Cracks*
*Sects and the City*
*Prince of a Thousand Worlds*
*Devil's Night*
*Portal-Land, Oregon*
*Stealing from Pirates*
*Fade to Gold*
*With a Broken Sword*
*Twice Against the Dragon*
*The House on Cedar Street*
*Sudden Death*
*On the Edge of Faerie*

**Short Story Collections**
*Spell Slingers*
*Twisted Timelines*
*Longhairs and Short Tales: A Collection of Cat Stories*
*Confronting Legends (Spells & Swords Vol. 1)*
*The Patreon Collection, Vol. 1-8 (Vol. 9, coming soon)*

**Nonfiction**
*The 30-Day Novel and Beyond!*

**Spells for Hire Series**
*Devil's Shoestring*
*Zombie Powder*
*Spirit Trap*
*Dragon's Blood*

**The Telepath Trilogy**
*Surviving Telepathy*
*Immoral Telepathy*
*Targeting Telepathy*

**Edge of Humanity Series**
*Caught Between Monsters*
*Hunting Monsters*

**Jumpstart Duchy Series**
*Into the Torn Kingdoms*
*The Dragon's Gold*
*The Gift Castle*
*The Deadly Feast*
*The King's Test*
*Triumph in the Torn Kingdoms*

Published by Thousand Faces Publishing, Portland, Oregon

http://1kfaces.com



Front cover image © Elena Kozyreva | Dreamstime.com (File ID: 101691373)



Hardback ISBN: 978-1-948490-42-9

Paperback ISBN: 978-1-948490-49-8

# THE OGRE OF THREEPEAKS

# PROLOGUE

One of the wonders of Lake Deepwater was that it was too deep to freeze, even in the heart of an Armyrian winter. Of course, in the opinion of Ser Ondine Ol'Natraz, that was also one of the lake's more disturbing features. Such depth lent credence to the rumors that it was bottomless.

Some even said that it was an open portal to another world. A world with no land nor sky nor sun, but only water. Endless water, and inhabited by those creatures of water known as "elementals" to the magically inclined.

Ondine, herself, had never been magically inclined. She was far happier with her sword in her hand and good, strong plate armor protecting her.

Magic always seemed too ephemeral. Which had to make it unreliable, didn't it?

Strange opinion to hold while in service to the duchy of Deepwater, where generations of Soulfist dukes and duchesses had been wizards, long before the new wizard-duke was raised up after Duchess Arinda died during the Godswalk Wars.

But none of the other knights ever faulted Ondine for her views. Nor did the duke himself, the one time she met him at Behal, to swear fealty. That large yellow diamond atop his white staff had been glowing with an uncanny kind of light in the dusky evening. And Ondine must've reflexively given that staff a distrustful look, because the duke laughed.

Not some kind of cold, arrogant-wizard laugh either. A simple, honest laugh of amusement, and maybe even understanding.

"Prefer torches, don't you?" he'd said, in that rich baritone of his. He even winked, like they were sharing a joke.

"I understand the light of a torch, your grace," Ondine had said carefully. "I..."

"It's all right, Ondine. You can tell him." That was from big, bearish Ser Beornric Ol'Sandallas, who was serving as the right hand of the duke.

Ondine had winced, but held steady and finished her point. "I always worry that a wizard's light shows only what the wizard wants me to see."

Ondine's guts tightened then, as the duke looked at her as though seeing through her. Which he might have been. She had no idea what the limits of his magic were. If any.

And given what he'd accomplished since then, she would have believed his magic had no limits at all.

But he hadn't censured her, or berated her, or even corrected her. He'd simply nodded.

"I've known a great many warriors who distrust magic," he'd said. "But none have ever phrased their concerns so succinctly or insightfully. I'm grateful to have you in my service, Ser Ondine. And I hope you can come to trust *me*, even if you distrust magic."

The duke had more than proven himself to her since then. In fact, it was her eagerness to please him that had gotten her into her current mess.

She could've waited for morning to leave on this mission. Crossed the lake by not much after midday, at the latest. Feeble warmth from that winter sun, but better than this.

No. Ondine had been eager to prove herself. And so she'd

combed the docks at Water's End for a ship that could take her out on the evening tides.

Only one such ship available for her. A sloop called the *Bright Idea*, that was heading home. Home, in this case, being Keljogran, at the northeastern tip of the lake.

Not as good, for Ondine's purposes, as going straight up the Golden river to Vabarett, in the county of Goldenfall. But with the wealthier folk only now heading home after the duke's wedding — a full aett after the event itself — all passage to Vabarett was booked solid for the next two aetts.

Still, the *Bright Idea* was fast, for a sloop. They'd reach the docks at Keljogran before midnight. It might even be possible for Ondine to find lodging for the night. Possibly even a tavern still open.

Something to give her one last break from the cold, before heading up for the mines among the Threepeaks Mountains.

Ah, well. At least it couldn't be much colder in Keljogran than it was out on the lake. Even here in this pitch-smelling cabin belowdecks, it was cold enough that Ondine paced to add a little extra warmth to the fading benefits from that tangy pork and ginger porridge she'd been given after boarding.

At least it wasn't snowing. There'd still be snow on the ground when she arrived, of course, but nothing was worse than getting snowed on while traveling at night.

Two bells before midnight, the *Bright Idea* put into port. The sailors were still settling their ship when Ondine walked her dark gray gelding, Blackflower, down the gangplank and onto docks that had seen better days.

Ondine was no sailor, but even she could tell that these docks needed repair. They looked as though someone had tried to destroy them during the wars, and half-succeeded. Repairs were underway, but they had quite a ways to go yet. Too much splintered or rotted wood. Too many missing or warped boards.

It was a wonder ships could still use this place at all.

Sadly, the footing wasn't much better even after she and Black-flower left the docks themselves. True, the cobblestones under her boots weren't likely rotting, but they were crusted with ice and no one had done all that much about clearing them of snow.

The streets were poorly lit, and by torches as often as lamps. With the feeble half-moon overhead doing little work of its own.

She'd have to mention conditions here, when she reported back at Water's End. That new duke seemed the type to want to know.

One benefit of all that snow, at least. Might've been chilling the air almost past tolerance, but it did reflect the light.

Unfortunately, not much of what Ondine saw around her gave her much hope. The nearby shadowed buildings all seemed closed up for the night.

The even chillier wind began to pick up. And just as she huddled into her cloak, despairing of finding any reasonable place to sleep, Ondine heard a combination of the sweetest sounds her half-frozen heart could imagine.

Music. Singing. Laughter.

She almost mounted Blackflower, in her haste to find this island of warmth and company in this otherwise desolate wasteland. But hooves, frozen cobblestones, and hurry formed the sort of combination that broke equine legs.

So Ondine settled for walking as fast as she felt was safe, leading Blackflower down two streets and over one more to find her haven. Three stories tall and lit up like it was still the Midwinter Festival. The sign out front depicted two unicorns — one black, one white — crossing horns.

Even better, this tavern — or maybe it was an inn — was large enough to have its own stables. With stablehands ready to take her horse. Stablehands with blankets, who knew how to handle a horse in vile temperatures.

Then, at last, Ondine pushed through the front door of — was it the Crossed Horns? The Double Unicorn? She wasn't sure what to call this place based on that sign — and into a world of light and laughter and best of all, heat.

Oh, but the fires in the twin hearths were roaring, as was the crowd of the common room. Singing something about a dragon and a man named Behal. Men and women aplenty filled the long bench tables. Humans mostly, but a scattering of tiny kindaren and huge, slate-gray na'shek.

But there was room for one more, and soon Ondine was warming herself inside with mulled mead and roast lake trout, served with an assortment of roasted root vegetables and a plenty of honeyed oat bread, while the fires and the company warmed the rest of her.

She even found herself singing along with "The Night the Bull Broke Loose," which was a ribald song she wouldn't even *admit* to knowing back in Water's End.

They were just reaching the verse about the bull breaking loose when a vaguely familiar voice rang out, "This version better include the farmer's son, or I'm doing my drinking elsewhere!"

The music stopped.

The singing stopped.

All the laughter and conversation stopped.

Over the sound of nothing but the whistling wind outside and the crackling twin hearths inside, the entire crowd turned to look at the newcomer.

She stood lean and lithe and smiling, clad in leathers of deep maroon. Her hair hardly much lighter in shade than her armor, and worn in a single braid down her back. At her belt, a rapier and dueling dagger.

Ser Deirdre Ol'Miri.

Arrogant, yes. Outspoken, undoubtedly. Annoying, quite often. But possibly the finest combatant Ondine had ever seen. In battle, she was both dancer and musician, providing performances unmatchable by any Ondine had ever heard of.

Ondine might not trust the magic of wizards, but the magic of dweomerblades like Deirdre was different. She didn't understand it, could never wield it, but she most certainly had learned to respect it.

To her surprise, the whole tavern erupted in cheers at Deirdre's arrival. Scattered men and women throughout the large main room began calling for her to join them.

Ondine couldn't understand it. She'd never seen *any* knight get a greeting like this one. This kind of greeting was usually reserved for popular musicians, especially skalds.

But a *knight*?

She turned to the smiling and shouting man next to her, who had the build and tan — and, alas, the odor — of a farmer.

"Why does Deirdre get this kind of greeting?"

He looked at Ondine as though she'd asked why the sun was rising in the east, instead of from some other direction.

"You don't know?" he gasped. Louder, to the *whole room*, he shouted, "We have a newcomer here! A knight who doesn't know the story!"

Ondine half-worried that they'd throw her out as some kind of infidel, but instead the crowd turned to Deirdre and began to chant.

"Tell it. Tell it. Tell it."

Over and over they chanted.

"Tell it. Tell it. Tell it."

Deirdre merely watched them with what could've been taken for polite interest, to any who didn't recognize the glint of pleasure in her jade green eyes.

Louder and louder, the crowd got.

*"Tell it. Tell it. Tell it."*

Finally, before they reached a frenzy, Deirdre raised her hands for silence.

The crowd stilled with impressive speed.

"Am I to understand," she said, clearly enjoying herself, "you wish me to tell a story?"

The crowd cheered.

"But which one?" She tapped a finger on her chin, as though considering. "My feats are so many and varied, I could tell stories straight through Midsummer and still not run out."

She shrugged helplessly. "What story do you want to hear?"

"O-gre! O-gre! O-gre!" The crowd chanted, and kept chanting until she raised her hands for silence again.

"Oh!" she said theatrically. "You want to hear the story of how I defeated the Ogre of Threepeaks! Is that it?"

The crowd roared approval.

"...And you want me to tell it when?"

"Now! Now! Now! Now!" They pounded the tables with their fists and the floorboards with their shoes and boots and feet as they chanted.

Deirdre called for silence once more, then with a deft flip, leapt up onto a nearby table.

"Someone will have to supply me ale or mead while I talk..."

A good two dozen tankards were hefted toward her.

"Better I have one of my own," she said, laughing. "And refills coming."

One of the serving men knew his cue. He stepped right up, and practically bowed as he handed a tankard up to her. She took a long quaff.

"Ah, much better. Bit nippy outside, you know."

It was an obvious joke, and yet they laughed. Ondine couldn't believe this.

"Now," Deirdre said, and the tavern — or inn, maybe — quieted around her. "I do believe it was this very night, not so many years ago, when the farms around here were losing good numbers of sheep and goats..."

# 1

———

Now, this was back in the days when I'd just reached the age of majority, and our illustrious new duke was still just an adventurous reprobate and not the fine pillar of nobility that he is these days.

Oh, I would have loved to have met him then. Bet we could've gotten into and out of all kinds of trouble together...

But that's neither here nor there. What matters right now, is that the story I'm about to tell you comes from the days when Duchess Arinda was still ruling Deepwater.

I'd been at Water's End for the Midwinter Festival, of course. You might quibble with the duchess over a point of policy here and there, or maybe over a tax issue, but she did throw some great parties. I tried never to miss them.

Unfortunately, those parties were sometimes a little too good, as the Festival had been that year. I don't think I'd been celebrating any harder than anybody else — or at least anybody else *capable* of properly celebrating an event like Midwinter...

(She coughed then, but Ondine was certain she heard the name *Yrsa* in that cough, referring to Deepwater's general, and the crowd laughed appreciatively.)

Excuse me. Guess my throat's still warming up.

Where was I?

Oh. Yes. Celebrating Midwinter properly. And, in fact, it was the morning after the kind of celebration that really warms a woman inside and out that I learned that my choice of bedmates had been...

Let's just say the choice wasn't *politically expedient*.

Couldn't regret it, though. Oh, what that man could do with his tongue. No wonder he was such a gifted speaker.

Anyway.

Point is, it turned out that the man I'd shared the noble privilege with that night had been the very man that *Duchess Arinda* had intended to invite to *her* chambers. Likely because she'd already known something about his skill at ... speechmaking.

Smart woman, the duchess.

Now, of course, half the point of the noble privilege is that we're not supposed to get upset about such things. And in her defense, the duchess didn't really get *mad* at me. But, well, she had this way of being frosty that was almost as bad. Side-effect of all that magic, maybe. When Arinda wasn't happy with someone, little things often started going wrong for that person. At least, so long as they remained at the Castle at Water's End.

Now, I've never been one to shy away from a challenge of any kind, and that includes magical. But there was another downside to getting my duchess and liege a little ... miffed at me.

See, hanging around the ducal courts have always been a certain number of powdered puffs who fail to appreciate me—

(Cue a round of disbelief from the crowd.)

I know, I know. I don't understand it either. Point is, any one of them might've taken advantage of my being out of favor. Maybe tried to persuade someone *in power* who didn't appreciate me — remember, that foul bastard Calder was still castellan in those days — that I'd ... violated an oath or something.

As if I'd do that! Please. I might not be the most ... respectful of knights — at least, when dealing with those who've done nothing to *earn* respect — but I take my oaths seriously.

So, rather than give my enemies the opportunity to strike with that foulest of weapons — politics — I figured the best thing I could do would be to clear out for a little while. Maybe take a lap of the lake, and return in an aett or two when the duchess had thawed toward me, and her court had other things to talk about.

So I gathered a pack, slung it over my shoulder, and started north along the shores.

("You didn't ride?" someone asked.)

In the dead of winter? With all that snow on the ground? I'd never subject a horse to that if I didn't have to. No, far better for me to go it on foot. And it would also take a little longer.

Besides, what did I have to fear from a little snow? A hot-blooded type like me? Weather that might've frozen some poor horse solid just felt no worse to me than a brisk summer breeze.

Unfortunately, the winter hunting along the shoreline isn't all that great. And because most people use the lake routes for travel, the towns have never been all that close together. So I don't mind admitting that I questioned the wisdom of my choice more than a few times over the first several days of my journey.

Why, I don't think I even ran across anything interesting before I reached Lachedran, where I'd somehow managed to get involved in a squabble between two lers who had more looks than land.

Now, how I solved that problem makes for a story that'd heat your blood on a chilly night like this one. Better that I not tell it tonight, though, as I do believe I see a few present who are still far enough below the age of majority that a proper telling would involve them learning things they *ought* to be learning from their parents. Or elder siblings. Or their friends.

Not from a scandalous knight in a tavern, anyway.

Suffice to say, though, that I ... resolved the problem between them, and that a ... happy ending was had by all. In fact, before the spring thaw, those two lers were married.

I swear. This world wouldn't have half its problems if people were honest with themselves and who and what they wanted.

Anyway, after Lachedran I encountered only points of minor

interest until I reached Keljogran. I'm sure some of you remember the problems you were having?

(The same three shouts from around the room. "Stolen sheep!" "Stolen goats!" "Stolen cattle!")

That's right. Your livestock was disappearing at an alarming rate. Well beyond anything that could've been attributed to the local wolf population. Or even the wider-ranging of the mountain cats.

And the way those fences had been broken, the way those thick, heavy rails had been snapped like twigs — plus those rather exceptionally large footprints left in the snow? A combination like that left few options about what the culprit could be.

("Ogres!" cried the crowd.)

Now, be fair. It *might've* been trolls. It wasn't until I'd already been in town a couple of days that your scouts came back and reported sighting an ogre, moving along the nearest slopes of the Threepeaks Mountains.

("So you wouldn't have faced trolls?" someone called out.)

Of course I'd've faced trolls. And they would've given me no more trouble than ogres. That strange trollish self-healing doesn't work when they're cut by *my* magical blades.

(Ondine expected the boastful knight to draw those blades and twirl them, or make them glow, or something equally flashy. Instead, she simply kept talking.)

But the techniques for *hunting* trolls are very different than the ones used for ogres. Also, in case you guys are ever plagued by trolls, you should know the only option is killing them. Or at least, killing *enough* of them that the others get the hint and go find someplace else to bother.

Trolls aren't big on negotiation or peaceful solutions.

Well, to be honest, ogres aren't exactly *known* for those things either. But every once in a while, you meet one smart enough to try talking *before* it tries to smash you into nice, easily digestible chunks.

Anyway, once your scouts confirmed for me what we were dealing with, well, then the question was what I should do about it.

For example, there are those who would insist that my *duty* as a sworn knight of this duchy was to carry this information back to my duchess at best speed. So that she could dispatch whatever force she decided was appropriate to handle the situation.

Me, though, I've never been the sort to pass on to others a problem I'd just as soon handle myself.

And since I wasn't exactly *in favor* at Duchess Arinda's court anyway, I chose to interpret my duty as requiring me to investigate and resolve the matter all on my lonesome.

(Here, for the first time, the bartender himself spoke up. "Bull shit!" he yelled. And Deirdre, rather than getting angry or offended, actually laughed. Heartily.)

You're right. Guilty as charged. I didn't once think about the duchess, or her court, or even what the technicalities of my duties would be in a situation like this one.

No, I didn't *need* to think about it to know I was about to head off into the mountains and deal with this ogre problem myself. And there were two reasons for that.

First, although I'd been here only a few days, that was more than enough to tell me what I needed to know about this town. You have good people here. You help each other. You pull together. Be proud of that. Not every town this size can say the same.

And second...

(Ondine scoffed as Deirdre broke into a grin.)

It sounded like fun.

**2**

———————

SOON AS I MADE IT CLEAR TO YOUR TOWN COUNCIL THAT I'D BE handling this little ogre problem myself, your people reaffirmed for me my conclusions about your goodness.

First, because you had volunteers ready to come along and help an ogre. That takes guts.

I have to admit, it was tempting to accept that help. I didn't know yet just how many ogres I'd be dealing with. And if the same thing happened today, I'd probably bring three or four of you along. Because I know that some of you are veterans of the Godswalk Wars, and have seen both battle and death.

(To Ondine's surprise, Deirdre actually got serious for a moment.)

Don't get me wrong. I'd be more than happy to see every one of you live a long, happy life without ever having to draw a weapon or stand to battle. And the less of violence and death that good people like you need to see, the better.

These things, they should be left to people like me. Knights. And to professional soldiers. And to the nobles who are worthy of their titles. Like our king, and our new duke.

We do these things so you don't have to.

(Deirdre raised her tankard then in a silent toast to the fallen.

Ondine raised hers as well, of course. Knights often made such a toast when drinking together. But to her surprise, the crowd of common folk all joined in the toast. With the kind of somber expressions that suggested that understood what they were toasting. And perhaps that they, too, had made this silent toast before.

After they drank, Deirdre continued in a lighter tone.)

At the time, though, the volunteers I was getting — even from your town watch, let's be honest here — might've had plenty of *willingness*, but no experience. Bringing them along would've done nothing but put them at risk.

(To Ondine's surprise, Deirdre didn't include the obvious second half of that statement. That bringing green troops along would've put *her* at greater risk as well. Maybe she considered it to go without saying.)

So I had to refuse the good people who wanted to help me. Which brings us to the second way your people reaffirmed their goodness for me.

I didn't even have to *ask* for supplies. Your farmers and butchers and bakers and crafters and others all practically fell over themselves to supply me for this venture. And when I tried to pay a fair price for the goods, *every single one* of you refused to take my money.

Every one of you.

You know, I've been thinking a lot about that, over the last year. Really, since King Colm raised up Aefric Brightstaff as our new duke.

Back when he was an adventurer, our duke often did things like I was doing that winter. He was famous for it. Finding out that a town was having problems with some monstrous foe, and going off into the wilderness to handle it.

And I imagine that he, too, often had to get supplies first from the very town he was going to help.

The way I figure it, those towns approached this in one of three ways.

First way, he wouldn't have to pay, because he'd be helping a town that could compete with this one for goodness. A town where the people would simply offer the man risking his life for them whatever he needed.

More often, I suspect, was a second result. The town council offered whatever he needed, and reimbursed those farmers and others for any goods they'd supplied him.

But sometimes ... sometimes I bet, that offer didn't come. Which meant he'd either have to *ask* for it, or he'd have to pay his own way.

Now, maybe some of those towns would've given him that support, if he asked. But from what I can tell of our duke, he never asked. Not even once. Just paid for whatever he could afford, and went without what he couldn't.

Imagine that. Just an itinerant adventurer. Sleeping on the ground more often than on even a cheap, straw bed. And a town who needed his help would make him pay to help them.

There are towns like that. I've been to them. Don't think much of the people who live in such places, and wouldn't be in such a hurry myself to help them out of a jam.

Our new duke though. I'll just bet that such an attitude didn't even cause him to hesitate. Even if it meant he'd be short-supplied, I'll bet he still went off to deal with their problems for them. Because he'd consider it the right thing to do.

He's just that kind of guy.

I should ask him about it sometime. Bet he'd have some fun stories to tell.

(The bartender spoke up again. "You didn't let us give you those supplies anyway!"

The room quieted around Ondine. Apart from a slight rumble of surprise, or maybe confusion. She wasn't sure which. Either way, this was clearly news to the crowd.

So Ondine watched Deirdre a little closer, trying to gauge her reaction. But Deirdre only looked sharply at the bartender, a solid, older man. She considered him for a moment.

Finally, she shook her head, smiling in exasperation. Sighed.)

Oh, I should not have brought this up. I forget you're still on the town council.

All right. It's true. I left enough—

("More than enough!" the bartender said.)

—Fine! *More* than enough to compensate your people for what I needed.

(The crowd around Ondine rumbled with ... was that distaste? Or just unhappiness?)

Look. It was a very generous offer, meant sincerely and coming from goodhearted folk. And I thank you all for it. I really do.

(That seemed to mellow them a bit, but from what Ondine could tell, these people still looked unhappy to learn that their generosity had been refused.

Deirdre continued anyway.)

But there was something your people weren't considering when they *made* that offer.

I was no itinerant adventurer. I was and am a sworn knight of the duchy you all happen to reside in. And even if that didn't give me a responsibility to help you — which it does — serving a duchy as rich as this one means I never lack for coin.

And even if, for some reason, my purse had been light that day. The nearest ler is ... what ... a half-day from here?

("Closer than that," the farmer next to Ondine called. "Doesn't take me *near* half a day to get deliveries to Ler Asktaina.")

Less than that, then. As a knight of this duchy, I could have required that ler's household to supply me for this mission. Same as I could any noble household from Kerrik Forest to the Risen Sea, and from the Dragonscar to the Merrek border.

Assuming, that is, that I were willing to take the time for such a trip, and that I put on a proper knightly smile and attitude.

(Even Ondine laughed at the way Deirdre rolled her eyes then. And the crowd positively ate it up.)

The point is, I had an obligation to help your people, a source of free supplies if I wanted it, and could more than afford to pay my own way. So I didn't need the generous offer of free supplies.

And yet, your people insisted on it anyway.

Well, I couldn't accept.

(The crowd grumbled.)

Look. Your economy was already taking a hit from the lost livestock. I had no intention of draining it any further, just for my own needs.

(That got some thoughtful sounds out of some of them, while they considered what she was saying.

Even more amazing to Ondine, though, was that Deirdre was making the effort to *persuade* them. As though she really *cared* what they thought. Ondine had never heard of Deirdre caring about what much of anybody thought. Apart from a handful of knights. Oh, and Duke Aefric, of course.

She seemed to care a great deal about what Duke Aefric thought of her...)

So, yes. I was grateful for the offer — and still *am*, by the way — and I appreciated what it meant for each and every one of you to make that offer. Nevertheless, as I slipped out of town that morning, I left ... a reasonable amount of money and a note where I expected that the town council would find both.

("You left them on the mayor's desk!" the bartender said. To Ondine's surprise, the whole common room burst into laughter at that. Ondine felt like she was missing something here...

Had the mayor's office been locked at the time?

No one asked, though. And Deirdre herself merely smiled and kept talking.)

Yes, well, I couldn't just leave them where just *anyone* could find them, could I. I mean, your *town* is full of good people. But that's no guarantee on the behavior of those who pass through.

No. I had to leave the money someplace safe. And obviously, I had to do it when no one was watching, or there might've been some argument and folderol, and it would've delayed my departure needlessly.

That would never do.

After all, I had to go see about this ogre problem.

**3**

———————

SO, WITH A FULL PACK AND A GOOD, FUR-LINED CLOAK, I SET OUT INTO the cold morning, just as the sun was beginning to crest the horizon. It was the kind of clear day that could almost make me believe I could see the ironwoods of Kerrik Forest, if I tried hard enough. Though of course, they're much too distant and too few to be visible from here.

Oh, I should mention. I'd been staying in this very inn, the night before.

(Aha! Ondine said to herself. This place *was* an inn, and not just a tavern. She'd have to see about getting a room for the night...)

And let me tell you, I've had the leftover-stew breakfast in more inns than I'd care to count. But they do it right, here at the Star Crossed Unicorns. Not sure what the cook does with the spicing — and I suspect she makes special sausages just to slice up and add to breakfast stew — but the result is delicious. Unless you have to catch the morning tide tomorrow, try not to miss it.

Anyway, that morning I remember the breakfast stew had been a particularly good combination of tangy broth and leftover chicken that contrasted wonderfully with the sharp, spiced sausage. Good enough that I mopped up the dregs with my honeyed oat bread.

And good enough to add a little extra bounce to my already fairly bouncy step as I set out into the snow after ogres.

Have to admit, the first part of that hunt was almost too easy.

I swear. Fight them sometime — or get hunted by them yourself — and you'll find out that, despite their size, ogres can be pretty stealthy when they want to be. But once they have their prey, it's like this extra helping of arrogance seeps into the blood. Makes 'em not care at all whether or not anyone can follow them.

So it was no trick to start at the latest sheep raid and follow a huge set of footprints across the snowy fields and hills right up close to the start of the Threepeaks Mountains.

I will say, though, that I did learn a couple of things along the way.

First, I was able to determine that the ogre responsible for the raids was between two and three times my height. Likely just about two-and-a-half times. Gauging that by the stride length between those footprints.

Which was a little trickier than it might have been, because of the second thing.

The ogre had been running. Not sprinting, of course, but loping along at the kind of ground-eating pace of someone used to long-distance running as their primary mode of transportation.

Why does that matter?

Because not all ogres can or do travel that way. A lot of them travel the same, sensible way we humans do, when covering long-distances on foot. They walk.

The ogres who can and do travel by that kind of running for extended periods of time are old enough to be out on their own, but not full adults yet. What we would call just about or just past the age of majority.

Adults, yes, but still figuring out what that means and how to establish themselves.

Kind of like I was at the time, really.

Now, I'd pretty much expected that we were dealing with an ogre of about that age, because that ogre kept coming *here* to raid. The ones that live long enough to reach what we might call a "respectable" age — and don't get me started on the differences between what Armyrians *do* consider respectable and what we *should* consider respectable — learn to space out their raids more. Draws less attention, and makes them less likely to find someone like *me* to coming to see about them.

And they don't want someone like me coming to see about them.

The smart ones don't, anyway.

The other thing I could determine from the fact that the ogre had been running was that its endurance would be pretty impressive.

Consider this. It had snuck down in the first place. From what your scouts had told me, it came down walking, at night, and moving from cover to cover until it got to its target destination.

Don't think that indicates intelligence, by the way. It's just the same level of cunning we might expect from any predator.

Point is, in sneaking down, the ogre likely took its time. Rested when it needed to. So let's just assume it was pretty fresh when it made its move. Nevertheless. That ogre sprinted the last distance to the farm, broke the rails it needed to break, brained three sheep and took off with them, running for its home in the mountains.

Which meant that the ogre had run for maybe half the night, carrying three sheep. And that ogre didn't take any breaks. Heck, to judge by the tracks, the ogre thief didn't even slow down until he reached one of the rockier slopes of the Threepeaks.

Only then did he or she slow to a walk, as they proceeded up and headed for what looked like a cave.

Pretty impressive, all told. Suggested that trying to tire the ogre out wouldn't be a very practical combat tactic.

For my part, I had no intention of pushing my endurance that hard. So it took me the better part of that first day just to reach the slopes leading up to that cave. After all, I wasn't running, and even if I had been, I didn't have the kind of stride that the ogre did.

It was getting on toward late afternoon at the end of a long hike when I reached the foot of that mountain, a few hundred feet from the cave I was almost certain that the ogre called home.

Now, someone less hot-blooded than me would probably have been driven to call it an early day. Would probably have felt an ache in all their muscles from hiking so far through the snow, on the kind of winter day where those clear skies just meant there were no clouds to hold in what little heat we got from the sun.

Yes, I imagine that a lot of people, in my place, would've given in to the temptation of rest and a fire, before going to see about that cave.

But me, well, if anything, that long hike had just gotten my muscles loose and warm. And my leathers had drunk up what little heat that afternoon sun had to offer me.

So with the prospect of a fight with an ogre only a short climb away, well, there was nothing for it but for me to make my way to that cave.

With any luck I'd finish off that ogre and make it back in time for a midnight supper.

You know, though. Even for me, things rarely work out *that* well.

**4**

———————

Now, one thing I had to give that ogre. He — or she ... or maybe they, I didn't know yet — had chosen well when it came to lairs. Whether that was a matter of good fortune, animal cunning, or actual intelligence remained to be seen, of course, but the point felt indisputable.

The cave was more than a hundred feet up a sheer rock face, with the only hand- and footholds spaced right for someone ogre-height. Hardly all that useful for someone of my stature. A fairly good way to avoid unwanted visitors in the late afternoon.

Oh. For those of you who haven't heard this story before, yes. I was certain that the ogre had gone into that cave. True, snow didn't exactly cling well to the rocky mountainside, so there were no obvious tracks to follow. But there was another tell my eyes were sharp enough to spot.

By the light of the late afternoon sun, I could pick out spots of sheep's blood here and there, near those hand- and footholds, on the way up to that cave. And none past it.

Yes, the ogre had gone into that cave. Might be in there right then, preparing its bounty of mutton. Waiting, unwittingly, for my arrival.

All I had to do to keep my intended appointment was reach that cave.

Now, I've been known to have an unkind word or two to say about wizardry from time to time — mostly about how the preponderance of its adherents are *theoreticians* who honestly believe they can *think* their way to the secrets of the universe without every leaving their precious *towers*. But I'll hand wizards this one.

They've got a spell that would've made reaching that cave a cinch.

Well, let's be honest here. They've got a couple of them. But the one I'm thinking of lets wizards — ones competent enough to merit discussion with good folks like yourselves, anyway — float straight up into the air, and even soar around like rocs or dragons, when they've a mind to.

(Ondine wasn't surprised to hear murmurs blending awe and disbelief from some of those around her, and reassurances and excited confirmation from those who'd witnessed such things themselves.

Ondine knew it was a fact that wizards could do fly, because she'd seen that new duke take off straight into the air with her own eyes. As, by now, had most of Behal and Water's End.

Deirdre was moving on, though.)

But in this case, I'm thinking of a spell of theirs I like the call "Fly on the Wall." Don't know what they call it themselves, of course, and I doubt it'll surprise any of you to learn that I don't much *care*, either. Especially since most of them probably call it something like "Some-such's Magnificent Gravitational Twisting" or "Blahdeblah's Vertic-ular Adherence."

Yeah, I'm not shy about my abilities. But those guys can get down-right *pompous*.

I like "Fly on the Wall." Descriptive. Practical. And not the kind of name that'd make anyone take themselves too seriously.

Anyway, point is, "Fly on the Wall" lets them crawl straight up walls and the like on their hands and feet, just the way flies will, with no particular worry about falling.

Yes, I freely admit that a spell like that one would've served me well that day.

(Deirdre handed her tankard to a serving man for a refill, while she tapped at her chin as though deep in thought. Which Ondine doubted very much. More likely, it was just a bit of showmanship, from a knight who dearly loved to be the center of attention.)

Which begs the question.

If I *myself* had such a spell, what do you think I would call it?

(Suggestions rang out around the common room. Most of them involving various insects and crawly things, but Ondine's favorite — not her own suggestion, of course, she didn't want to play into Deirdre's games — was also the one that sent the room into peals of laughter.

"Ser Deirdre's Spell of Guaranteed Bedroom Access!"

Deirdre joined in the laughter, and toasted the suggester when the serving man presented her a full tankard.)

It would be that, wouldn't it? I can think of a bedroom or two I wouldn't mind being able to crawl in and out of unseen. The noble privilege can be a wonderful things, sometimes.

But I understand that you folk have your own equivalent to that practice these days. Or has it not spread to a town as small as this one?

(Several voices called out that it had, with one woman in the corner being especially loud and enthusiastic in her cry of, "Oh, yes it has! And thank Ulna!"

Ondine wondered about that a little. Yes, the discovery of the contraceptive value of nysta tea — when drunk by either sex — had opened up options and led to the nobility eventually deciding that issues of jealousy and unrequited mutual desire had caused more problems than land and water rights combined. But did the common folk have as many problems brought on by such things? Or was it simply a matter of them emulating their nobles?

Not something she could get an answer to easily, alas.

And anyway, Deirdre's own suggestive laughter was easing down, and there might yet be hope that she'd get back to her story.)

I should've known. Thought some of you looked especially well-satisfied. Might even explain why you're all so quick to come to one another's aid.

Well, good on you. Hope it brings you folk as much pleasure as the noble privilege brings us.

Anyway, I wasn't talking about bedrooms I've been in over the years—

("I could stand to hear a few stories about those," a man called from one table over, which brought some appreciative laughter from the crowd, though not as much as Ondine might've expected.

One of the rules of the noble privilege, after all, was that nobles only slept with other nobles. And knights might share the bottom rung of nobility with lers, but they were still nobles.

For one of them to get *too* flirty with Deirdre would be inappropriate, and might spoil an otherwise fun evening.

Fortunately, Deirdre ignored the comment and pushed on.)

Instead, I was talking about hunting down that ogre, and how I got up to his cave on that sheer, rocky mountainside.

Now, I didn't have any of those wizard spells to help me. But us dweomerblades, we have our own magics that can help us out in ... oh, let's just all them strategically important moments.

And this one definitely counted.

So I recalled a technique from the early days of my training.

You see, dweomerblades are *called* dweomerblades because the first of us — those who established us as unique from both fighters and other magic-users, centuries ago — all focused their power through swords and daggers of various sorts.

Not because our magic is *limited* to blades. Some of us use maces, flails, axes, spears, and so on. And most of us can also channel our power through arrows or bolts we fire from bows or crossbows.

But the truth is, we don't strictly *need* such weapons at all to use our magics.

(To Ondine's amazement, Deirdre's hands and fingers became limned in a reddish glow as she held them up to demonstrate.)

We first learn to channel our power through our bodies.

(The glow went away.)

And in the early days of my training, I figured out how to use that power for more than just an edge in a fight.

I learned how to make my own hand- and footholds in stone and wood.

Well, wood's a little trickier, actually. If I cut a groove in stone this way, it's just the groove I want. But with wood, sometimes the borders ... expand on me. Or part of the wood snaps. Or it splinters. Makes the technique much less reliably a tool for this sort of climbing.

But up a sheer rockface? Well, I won't say it was *too easy*, but it wasn't all that hard for me to cut my own grooves, for my fingers and the toes of my boots.

Nothing too deep. That require too much work, while suspending myself over a drop. But not too shallow, either, or I'd slip. I had to make the holes just broad enough to fit a decent portion of boot inside, so I could divide my weight and most swiftly.

But as you can probably guess, I've done this more than a few times over the years. No, I won't tell you where and when. Girl's got to have *some* secrets.

(Ondine rolled her eyes as the crowd laughed appreciatively.)

All told, this technique allows someone as nimble as I am to scurry up a little more than a hundred feet of rockface without too awful much trouble. Which was just what I did.

Then I reached the cave, and the hunt began in earnest.

## 5

———

IT WAS DEFINITELY AN OGRE-SIZED CAVE. TOP HAD TO BE ... THREE OR four times my height. And it was broad across as ... maybe half this common room.

(That brought a round of murmuring from the crowd, though Ondine couldn't tell about what. Or even why this was worthy of note. Of course it had to be an ogre-sized cave, or no ogre would use it.)

Cave floor was rocky and dusty, and littered here and there with the bones of small animals. Nothing big enough to be a sheep or pig or cow. Definitely not a cow. But vermin-sized. Voles and birds, I thought. Picked clean, with clear teeth marks from where they'd been gnawed at. Old enough and yellowed enough that there wasn't even much smell to them.

And I could tell that, because this cave didn't look or smell like an ogre's home.

An ogre's home smells... Well, we'll get to that later. But the point is, this cave mouth didn't smell much worse than most other cave mouths. And yes, I've had to camp in a few.

This one had that dry, dusty, rocky smell mostly. Couldn't pick up any wet scent in here — so I didn't think it was what miners call a live cave.

No. That's not right. *Living* cave. That's right, isn't it?

(Ondine shook her head and sighed at the obvious play to the crowd. But they ate it up, and shouted that she was right.)

Good. I thought so.

Funny turn of phrase, though. Living cave. I mean, if anyone said that outside of a mining context, I'd probably think they meant that the cave itself was alive. Maybe had stalactites and stalagmites as teeth.

(Most of the crowd sounded dismissive, but one of the few na'shek stood up. And when something that big, tall, and slate gray stands up, the humans and kindaren in the room all turned to see what she'd say.

This na'shek was wearing one of those togas they favored. Ondine wasn't sure how they beat some kind of stiff cloth out of rock, but that was how they were supposedly made. Certainly the colors were right. Dark reds and oranges.

The na'shek woman spoke the Common Tongue, but slowly and in a deep, yet undeniably feminine, voice.

"Ser Deirdre is right to suggest such a thing. There are caves that live. That breathe. That think. There are entire mountains that live. Your human miners should find another term. That one is … disrespectful."

The crowd murmured displeasure, and for a moment Ondine thought that things might get ugly.

There were only five na'shek, and a whole lot more humans. But na'shek had size and strength on their side. And their skins didn't cut as easily as humans'…

Deirdre let loose a sharp whistle, getting everyone's attention.)

I can guarantee you that no one means any disrespect by the phrase. I've spoken to more than a few miners over the years, and one thing they all have in common is a deep respect for the mines and the mountains themselves.

And let's be fair, here. This is hardly the time, the place, or the audience to suggest an entire profession change one of its accustomed phrases.

(The na'shek woman frowned, then slowly nodded. But just before she sat down again, Deirdre said something in Na'shese. Ondine didn't understand it, but she did pick out the word *renkat*.

Whatever she'd said, it must've been a joke, because all five na'shek burst into surprised laughter.)

Ah, dirty jokes play in every language.

Now, back to what I was saying.

Point is, the cave smelled dry. Dusty. And cold as it was, the smell of that ogre hadn't lingered. I couldn't even smell any trace of the dead sheep.

In fact, I might've second-guessed myself about where the ogre had gone, except for one thing.

There wasn't a lot of snow in here. And what snow there was had had great scoops taken out of it. Say, for melting down and drinking, or for cooking. Scoops that hadn't been taken with a pot or a bowl, but with a hand.

A very big hand.

So I was in the right place. I knew that much right from the entrance. But to find the ogre, I'd have to go deeper. Into the shadows and growing darkness. Because outside, yeah, the sun would still be giving enough light to see by for ... oh, at least another hour or so. But here in this cave, the angle was wrong. Sunlight was streaming *past*, not *into*.

I had a solution for that. But first, I crouched where I was and listened.

Easiest things to hear were the wind past the cave entrance, and the cries of a few hawks in the distance. Unless I was mistaken, I thought it was late in the day for hawks to still be hunting. I wondered if it was related to the ogre...

That was just a thought to cook at in the back of my mind. Most of my attention was on listening. Trying to focus past what I could hear easily.

In this case, that meant listening past the wind, mostly. The way it whistled nearby almost nonstop. But I couldn't go into those shadows until I knew I wasn't missing some important sound, under that whistling wind.

Perhaps the soft footfall of a sneaking ogre. Or perhaps the heavy, anticipatory breaths of an ogre hiding in ambush.

But I couldn't hear either. Not from where I was.

No choice for it, then. I'd have to push on, and hope the ogre wasn't lying in wait for me.

Mind you, I didn't see how he could be. I wasn't making much more noise than my shadow, so no way he could have heard me. And unless he'd happened to be looking down from the cave as I approached the mountain, he couldn't have seen me either.

Smelled me, maybe? Smelled my sweat? My leathers? My ... humanness?

That was a possibility I had to consider. I'd never been too sure just how sensitive the ogre nose was. I mean, sure, to *me* their stench was so bad I couldn't imagine how they could smell cooking meat at two paces. But they had to *live* with that stench. So maybe they'd learned to tune it out, the way we can tune out a repetitive noise.

Like a smith's hammer, during the day. You only notice it when it's missing.

So I had to figure there was a chance he'd smell me coming. But there wasn't much I could do about it. So I'd just have to stay ready.

I drew my blades. Not just because I'd want them in hand if there *was* an ambush coming, but because that reddish glow? The one you all saw around my hands a few minutes ago?

Yes. About that. It's not very showy, I know. It's dim, and not all that easy for most of you to see in this well-lit establishment. Truth is, you wouldn't see much more, even by dim lamplight or starlight.

But for me, that soft glow sheds light as well as any lantern. Lets me see clearly out to about ... fifteen, maybe twenty paces, depending on conditions. Then it dims like any light. Which means I see dimly for maybe another ... eight, ten paces?

Something like that. I've never felt the need to measure it precisely. I leave that sort of dithering to the wizards.

So with my blades aglow, I moved forward as quietly as I could. Which is considerably, if I say so myself.

The cave didn't go back all that far. Maybe ... a hundred feet? Something like that. But even over that distance, I saw more than a few signs that the ogre had, in fact, been here more than a few times.

Stalactites snapped in half, with their tips scattered across the cave floor. Stalagmites that had clearly been broken off at the root by a heavy kick.

Wanton destruction. Done by something bigger and stronger than a borog or na'shek.

Well ... obviously a *na'shek* wouldn't needlessly damage stalactites or stalagmites, but you get my point.

Actually, let me explain a little here. Because despite my warnings that you folk shouldn't go hunting monsters on your own — and really, you *shouldn't* — I know full well that there are always those with more courage than sense.

(Ondine had to stop herself from saying, "Like you?" She got as far as having the breath drawn and her lips parted before her eyes reminded her that this crowd — though it liked to tease — was *firmly* on Deirdre's side.

Not the best place to say something that could be construed as an insult.

Largely, because it would have been an insult.

Fortunately, Deirdre pushed on.)

And in case a few of that type are present, here's something to remember.

Wanton destruction — like with those stalagmites and stalactites in the cave — is a clear sign that you're dealing with an ogre.

Giantfolk, even young ones, don't go in for wanton destruction. It goes against their innate sense of artistry, which runs *deep* in giants. From speech to construction to just about anything else, if giantfolk do it, they'll treat it as high art.

So if you see wanton destruction that requires something bigger than, say, a borog, it's not a giant.

And despite what you may have heard, it's not likely a troll either.

Don't get me wrong. Trolls don't have anything *against* wanton destruction. They just don't *care*. An ogre'll break things like that just to break them. To feel the contact, and reassure itself of its might.

Trolls don't think that way. They don't eat the rock, so they don't bother the rock.

Trolls are pretty much all about their stomachs.

Now, back to the hunt.

As I moved through the cave, I found more bones. Most of them not worth mentioning.

One set, though.

They were broken up. Not an intact skeleton. But more like, well, more like they'd been parted out for easier consumption. And not only had they been gnawed on — by larger teeth than had gone at those birds and vermin — some of the bones had been broken. Likely to get at the marrow.

These were human bones.

Yeah.

Any tiredness I might've been feeling, that went right out the cave mouth.

And I was suddenly thinking that I wasn't so interested in the possibility of *talking* with this ogre.

# 6

So I was a little more grimly determined now, as I reached the back of that cave. Seeing those human bones drove home the threat the ogre now presented to the local populace.

Problem is — and this goes for trolls, as well as ogres — once an ogre's tasted the flesh of a human ... or a kindaren, or derekek, or na'shek, or eldrani ... they'll never again be satisfied with animal flesh. Not for long, anyway.

This isn't speculation, either, in case some of you might be thinking that I'm just saying that to add a little more tension to my story.

(Ondine looked away guiltily.)

I'd been told this about ogres during my training, by no less than *Ser Carinoch Aldwema* himself.

(That brought a respectful buzz from some of those present, but not all.)

For those of you who don't know the name, Ser Carinoch is called "Ogrebane" down around the Free Baronies of Olwich, and the great Forest of Dellwood. A name he'd more than earned *years* before he trained me.

Wasn't just his opinion, either. In the years since, I've talked about ogres with other knights, as well as with a few of those who've survived a life of adventurous mischief to find themselves rewarded with titles. Like our own dear duke, long may he live, and others as well. Countess Faenella, for example. Not sure how many of you know this, but Fyretti's new countess is of the order of Blessed Knights, and used to travel with an adventuring band of her own.

And I'm sure you all know that up north in Silverlake, their duke was once an adventurer. That was decades ago, of course, though he still wears those old blades of his. And he has quite a roguish smile, when you get him talking about his youth. Oh yes, I've discussed ogres with Duke Wylyn.

Everyone I've talked to, they all say the same thing. Once an ogre tastes the flesh of one of Qorunn's sentient races, it becomes a craving for them that no mere animal can satisfy.

So yes, this one might've just hunted for sheep. But I was now willing to bet that those sheep were meant to fortify that ogre while he or she studied the nearby towns. Trying to find the easiest towns-folk to snatch for the stewpot.

Honestly, knowing that this was now the case, I regretted one thing about the way I'd gone about my mission. I regretted that I hadn't sent a rika to Water's End first, informing the duchess about the ogre and telling her that I was handling it.

No, not to brag to the duchess, if that's what you're thinking.

(Ondine was, in fact, thinking that, and felt a little guilty about it. She also started wondering if Deirdre could read minds.)

I wasn't worried about getting back into Duchess Arinda's good graces. No. I knew time would be enough to take care of that.

I wanted to send that rika in case I failed.

(Silence spread through the inn's common room, until the only sounds came from the kitchen and the hearth fires. Deirdre's next words were quiet.)

Not that I thought I *would* fail. I never had before, and haven't since. But the kind of failure I'm talking about only happens *once*. And only a fool thinks they'll get advance warning of when that failure will come.

Whether I wanted to admit it or not, I knew there was a *chance* that I'd die while trying to end the threat of this ogre. And if I did, without that rika, it might take time before word of my death reached your townsfolk. Time that would be wasted, before the bad news reached the duchess. Before she could get someone else out here to deal with this threat.

A delay that might cost someone else their life.

A delay that would be my fault.

(The bartender spoke up then. "The mayor sent that rika, Ser Deirdre. The very morning that you left. Duchess Arinda would've been told by the time you reached the back of that first cave.")

Really?

(To Ondine's great surprise, Deirdre started laughing. Her laugh was infectious enough that some others got caught up in it, even though Ondine doubted very much that those people knew why they were laughing.

Ondine certainly didn't get the joke.)

That is *so* like her grace. You see, she never told me. Because there was never a *need* to tell me. I'd lived. I'd taken care of the threat. So her grace acted in such a way that I wouldn't find out she'd sent some kind of backup team.

She had that kind of subtlety. And she never did *anything* that could be construed as undercutting or even simply *not trusting* her knights.

So far as the world was concerned, she'd been told that I would handle it and simply assumed my success.

(Deirdre toasted the late duchess then, and the whole common room joined her. But after the toast, the bartender spoke up, puzzled.

"But, Deirdre, Duchess Arinda *did* trust you. She never *sent* a backup team.")

Oh, no? Tell me. Did any party of knights pass through here a day or two later? Maybe with orders to act as surveyors of some kind? Or perhaps to check on the state of things at the mines? Or maybe on their way to...

(Deirdre trailed off, smiling, and Ondine noticed that the bartender's eyes had widened.

"A team came through the next day," he said. "On their way to check on the mines."

Ondine shook her head, irritated that Deirdre had been proven right. After all, that was the same mission she was on. And it certainly didn't require a *team*.)

Exactly. And they probably found an excuse to linger here a couple of days. Or maybe moved to another town closer to the mines, but still close enough to see if I returned in a timely fashion.

("They lingered here." The bartender shook his head. "Just happened to leave the day scouts spotted you returning. Didn't even occur to me — to *any* of us — that the timing of their leaving wasn't a coincidence.")

Likely they rode for Lachedran and caught the next ship back, with no one but themselves and a few of her grace's most trusted advisers ever knowing what their true mission had been.

I'm glad, though. Glad to know that my impulsiveness wouldn't have cost this good town, if I'd failed.

Either way, there in that cave on that cold, late afternoon, I didn't know any of this. So I regretted my arrogance in not sending the message myself.

And I redoubled my determination to end the ogre, before anyone else died.

My steps a little surer now, I reached the back of that first cave.

There were two tunnels leading out of it. Neither one looked entirely natural to me. A little too regular. But their edges didn't look to have been *worked* either, the way most miners — including you na'shek — would have worked them. The walls were still rough, with enough projections and inconsistency that I could almost believe they were natural.

But the height and width were too regular.

I didn't know this then, but that's how borogs tunnel. They have a relationship with stone that's not like anything else I've ever seen. It's not the same as the na'shek relationship, obviously, but in its own way, it's just as sacred.

(The na'shek grumbled, unhappy to hear a tone of admiration in Deirdre's voice when discussing *anything* about their ancient enemies. And honestly, Ondine wasn't all that thrilled with it herself.

But Deirdre had probably met those borogs the duke had allowed to live up in the Dragonscar, while Ondine, herself, had not. So maybe there was reason for a measure of praise here?)

Moving on, my point is, at the time, I thought the ogre might've done some work on those tunnels. Which was concerning. Made me think this one might be smarter than I'd been led to expect, from ogres.

Ogres already have strength and toughness on their side. If they started getting smarter, they could become a real problem.

Well...

A real problem once one of them figures out how to organize the others. Until that day, even the occasional *smart* ogre won't have a long lifespan, unless he or she uses those smarts to avoid doing things that bring people like me after them.

In the meantime, I was looking at two tunnels, but only trying to find one ogre. Which meant I had to figure out which tunnel was the right one.

Now, I *could* tell you that I spotted some trace of sheep blood. Or maybe used some fancy dweomerblade trick to figure out which tunnel was the right one. *If* I were the sort of person to exaggerate her own abilities. Which, of course, I'm not.

When you're as awesome as I am, you don't need to exaggerate.

(Ondine *wanted* to feel an urge to be sick, but had to admit that Deirdre's reputation was — to the best of her information — very well earned. And reinforced with annoying regularity.)

So the truth is, I picked one at random.

Well, not *quite* at random. I mean, there was a *bit* of logic to it. Best as I could tell, that ogre was carrying the sheep with its right hand. Figuring that maybe meant a preference, I guessed the right-hand tunnel and followed it.

Wasted more than an hour down that damned tunnel. And its little side tunnels. But there was nothing to be seen in there, except a few perfectly natural critters, living among the remnants of some people who'd lived there a very long time ago.

Borogs, likely, given what I've learned about them since. Didn't know that at the time, though.

In other words, I didn't find the ogre down that right-hand tunnel.

So I had to retreat back up to the first cave and try the other. That left-hand tunnel.

And, in the kind of amusing happenstance that one comes across in life, as long as one lives well, the *left* tunnel turned out to be the *right* choice.

# 7

---

(Fortunately, Ondine wasn't the only one in the crowded common room of the Star Crossed Unicorns Inn who groaned at Deirdre's awful — and obvious — excuse for a joke. Because if she had been, she probably would have left. No point in feeling *that* alone amidst a crowd, no matter how cold the night outside.

Less pleasing, though, was the number of people who actually laughed.

Then again, the ale and beer had been flowing pretty freely. So Ondine reassured herself that anyone who laughed at *that* sad little joke was drunk enough to laugh at anything.

Worse, Deirdre, if she even noticed all the groans, seemed only amused by them. Or maybe even encouraged. Well ... at least she didn't have another one nocked and ready to loose. Rather, she just pushed ahead with her story.)

I'd gone no more than maybe ... three score paces down that left-hand tunnel before I realized that the signs that the ogre had gone this way were obvious, now that I thought about it.

All those little forms of life I'd found in the right-hand tunnel? Rats and voles and spiders and millipedes and such?

I hadn't run across any of them so far. Not living, anyway. What few spiders I found had been squished flat, whether they'd been on the ground, the walls, or even the roof of the tunnel.

Poor little things had probably moved at the wrong time and found themselves on the wrong end of the ogre's impulse for wanton destruction.

Tunnel curved a couple of times, and I even passed three openings leading into what I could think of as chambers. None of them held any ogres, though the ogre had lived in one of them for a time. I could tell that by the dead vermin, and the lingering smell of ogre.

Well, I guess I can't put this part off any longer. Hope nobody's eating.

(A few people were, but they put down their forks and spoons while Deirdre continued.)

Ogres blend a few odors kind of like the ones that most people would recognize. Musk ox is the most pleasant of these, and might even dominate, if they ever bathed. But they don't. And the worse smells are more like rancid meat and offal, combined with the ripe dung and piss of a very unhealthy person.

(Ondine had smelled worse — or at least things as bad as that — on battlefields. But she was glad she'd finished her own meal before contemplating those smells again.)

Each of those smells alone can be bad enough. But when you smell them in combination, that means you're too close to an ogre.

That smell was pretty faint in the chamber I'd found. Made me think it had been quite some time since the ogre had been in here.

Which made me take a closer look at it.

Only maybe ... four paces across and deep, with a ceiling not much more than twice my height.

Too small, in other words, for the ogre I was chasing. At least, at the ogre's current size. Made me reconsider the way those small animals in that first cave had been gnawed down to the bones.

I started to think that this ogre had lived here quite a while before anyone learned of it.

Thing is, that suggested that the ogre had been quite young when first moving into these tunnels.

So where were Mommy and Daddy?

With an ogre, there were several possibilities.

If I'd been dealing with a troll, Mommy and Daddy would definitely have been around there somewhere. Trolls don't eat each other. In fact, other trolls are just about the only creatures that trolls *won't* eat. Don't know why that is.

Ogres, though, they vary pretty widely. Some consider their families important enough to keep together, which is about the only way you ever find ogres in groups. They don't trust each other enough to form tribes or clans or anything.

Some ogres, though, consider even their own family to be competing for resources. And would either drive them off or kill and eat them.

Considering that livestock hadn't been disappearing *too* fast, odds were that I was dealing with an ogre who'd been kicked out by his parents. Who probably lived somewhere else among the Threepeaks, and contented themselves with mountain goats and the like.

But I didn't know that for sure. I had to consider the possibility that those parents were around here somewhere.

So when I went back into the tunnel to continue my hunt, I took a little extra care to be stealthy.

Sneaking around is pretty easy in short bursts. But try doing it for a whole afternoon without slipping up once. I bet even your local hunters catch themselves slipping sometimes, when the hours of the hunt grow long and they haven't really taken a break.

Had I slipped up at all to that point? I didn't know. I *couldn't* know, almost by definition. I mean, unless you snap a twig — or where I was, kick some loose rock — when you're trying to sneak you can't really judge how well you do it.

*You're* going to hear any little sounds you make, but that doesn't mean anyone else will hear them.

They *might* though. Because you can't be one hundred percent sure how far those little sounds will carry. Or who might be listening at *just* the wrong moment for you.

That's why I mentally redoubled my effort on sneaking. Trying to make up the difference with focus, without losing too much attention on the tunnel ahead of me.

Wouldn't do to focus on my own stealth to the point that I missed a big freaking ogre with its club raised, just because it happened to be standing still.

Anyway, after a couple more bends and empty, unused chambers, I came to a split. This time I spotted some sheep's blood on the right-hand branch, and knew it was the right direction.

I was starting to feel the cold now. The sun had to have set by this point, and while I did have a great many tons of rock and dirt around and above me, which by all rights should have warmed things a little, the tunnel was big enough and open enough that any natural heat just slipped away.

And sneaking like that, it wasn't doing enough to keep my limbs limber. My adrenaline from the start of the hunt had faded some, and so I'll admit that even my hot blood wasn't doing enough to keep me warm.

I was shivering more than a little. And that I hadn't smelled any smoke, by now, suggested that the ogre didn't have a fire going. Wasn't like he could have cut himself a chimney, after all.

So I tried to console myself that the ogre was cold too, and I made my way down that right-hand tunnel.

And after only another ... thirty paces or so, I smelled something that got my blood pumping again.

Not smoke. Ogre. I was getting close.

**8**

———————

I WAS MOVING THROUGH A ROCKY, YET STRANGELY REGULAR TUNNEL, maybe three of my paces across, and maybe about twice my height. Might've been the smell of water to the air now — I was certainly deep enough that likely there was water dripping *somewhere* — but that smell got drowned out by the foul stench of ogre.

And remember. Up to this point, I'd been sneaking through the darkness, on my hunt. I hadn't lit any torches or lanterns, that someone else might see.

No, *I* was able to see thanks to the faint red glow that limned my naked rapier and dueling dagger. Light that provided more than well enough for me, but wouldn't attract notice as readily as a torch or lantern would.

And the less said about those bright light-ball spells that wizards use, the better. Might be great for studying musty tomes late into the night, high up in a tower somewhere, but *useless* for moving about unseen in the darkness.

Soon enough, though, I began to realize that my weapons were no longer providing the only light.

Ahead of me down the tunnel, I could see the glow of what looked for all the world like firelight.

I didn't see how that could be. I wasn't smelling any smoke, and if there was a fire, I should have. I should have smelled a lot of it. Because I *had* to be approaching along the easiest path for that smoke to take out of the mountain.

A torch maybe? With a high enough ceiling, the scant smoke from a torch might not come my way.

In either case, fire meant I was approaching *some*one. Had yet to come across any naturally occurring fires inside a tunnel that wasn't part of a volcano.

(One of the na'shek started to stand up, but Deirdre waved him to sit back down with a chuckle.)

Oh, I'm sure there are ways that fires just *happen* inside a mountain. And I'm equally sure that our na'shek friends here could list them *all* for us. But that list isn't germane to my story, so if you don't mind, let's just stick to what *I* knew while I was in that tunnel. Sound good?

(To Ondine's surprise, Deirdre actually gave the na'shek a moment to consider, and they discussed the question quietly among themselves, in Na'shese. Finally, the one who'd started to stand turned and gave Deirdre a rather dramatic nod to go ahead.)

Thank you.

Now. There I was, in that cold, rocky tunnel, seeing what had to be firelight ahead. Firelight that implied to me that I'd found someone. Most likely the ogre, but I didn't know that for sure yet.

And I needed to know more before I took another step closer. I needed to know all I could figure out.

Now, deep inside the mountain as I'd gone at this point, the distant sounds of birds and wind had faded to nothing. The only sounds I'd heard for ... oh, at least the better part of an hour ... had been sounds *I* made. My breathing. My heartbeat. The soft sounds of my stealthy footfalls.

So first, I tried to eliminate my own sounds.

Stopped moving.

Held my breath.

Calmed my heartbeat.

And ahead of me...

Yes.

I heard movement. Heavy movement. Heavy enough to be the ogre. And occasional rumbles that might have been that kind of pidgin Common Tongue that some of them could handle for language.

And under that, I swear, I heard what had to be the crackle of a fire. Not a torch. A fire. Which irritated me, because how could there be a fire without smoke I could smell?

I started moving again, as quietly as I could.

And soon the sound of that fire was supported by something even more irritating.

I smelled what had to be roast mutton.

Poorly spiced roast mutton, with an under-smell that I didn't care for. But then, ogres had never been noted for their culinary mastery.

My focus, though, wasn't on the smells of the cooking or the irritating possibility of a smokeless fire. It was on those occasional attempts at speech.

Those implied that the creature wasn't alone.

Prisoner, maybe? Or a second ogre?

I wasn't sure which would be worse.

I let the glow fade from my weapons, and stopped moving again while my eyes adjusted. The distant glow didn't give me much visibility, but that didn't worry me. The walls of these tunnels might've been inconsistent, but their floors had been uniformly reliable.

Besides, I'd never heard of an ogre laying a tripwire, or other kind of trap. They were too likely to forget they'd done it and fall victim to it themselves.

Slowly and quietly, I slipped through the darkness, until I finally reached the edge of the chamber ahead.

Now *this* was an ogre-sized chamber. Had to be a score, maybe two dozen strides across. Maybe a little more than that, even.

Round, it was, and surprisingly even along the walls.

Ceiling high enough that it faded into the shadows.

And that ceiling had to have some kind of vent. Because sure enough, the smoke was going straight up from a fire in the middle of the chamber. A fire big enough to keep an ogre warm. Hells, I could feel its warmth from my hiding place in the tunnel. And I can't deny that that warmth felt welcome, after so many hours in the cold.

The stench, of course, was a lot less welcome.

Not quite overpowering, thanks to the roasting mutton — all three of those sheep, roasted whole on a big spit — but still, far too much of that awful odor. That stench of rancid meat and offal, combined with ripe, unhealthy dung and piss.

Had to fight not to gag on that stench. Couldn't give myself away now.

Because the ogre himself was in there.

Three times my height, he stood. Wore a kind of toga vaguely stitched together from mountain goat hides, that slung up over one shoulder and fell down to about his knees.

And it *was* a he, to judge by the scraggly beard, that was just as dark and greasy as his long black hair.

And that's not all.

Ogre skin, it's not like what you and I think of as skin. It's more like a hairless kind of hide. It's mottled. And this one's main color was kind of bruise-purple, with irregular splotches of a sickly greenish tinge.

His eyes were that same greenish color, with slanted horizontal pupils. Like a goat has.

He had built a kind of bed near the fire, from the skins of more goats. Which made me wonder. Why had the ogre not skinned those sheep? Clearly he was adept enough at skinning goats.

Then again, I didn't see any blade anywhere. I could see a club, which was little more than a felled sapling with the branches broken off. Probably as long as I was tall.

But I didn't see any kind of knives or swords around.

Odd.

If the ogre hadn't skinned those goats, who had? And how had the ogre gotten them?

Trade?

That would suggest that this ogre was indeed smart. For an ogre, anyway. And there was another sign that could be taken as intelligence.

He was alone. I couldn't see, hear or smell anyone else in this chamber. And yet, sometimes he did speak to himself.

"'ree gars. Setter."

Kept saying that over and over. Like he was contemplating it. And since I didn't see anyone in immediate danger, I stayed hidden for a bit while I tried to figure out what the ogre meant by those words.

Not sure how long it took me, but this is what I concluded.

*'ree* was his way of saying *three*. And *gars* meant *guards*.

Once I had those, I figured that *setter* had to be *sunset* or *center*. And sunset made more sense to me. He'd studied his next target enough to know that after sunset he'd have to deal with only three guards. Or maybe, that three guards changed shift at sunset.

Either way, he was planning his next attack already.

And it was time to let him know I was here.

**9**

———————

Now, tactically speaking, I'm sure most of you are thinking that the smartest way to fight that ogre would've been to draw him to me. To stay just inside the entrance to the tunnel, where I had full freedom of movement, but where there wasn't enough room for him to swing his club.

(Ondine nodded reflexively. She certainly would've preferred that. And others around the common room made little sounds of agreement.)

But there were two problems there.

First, this ogre clearly had some smarts to him. Which meant he'd see what I was doing and not bother with his club. More likely he'd grab a couple of burning logs — and he was, in fact, burning wood, as opposed to, say, dung — and come after me with those. Or kick at me with those massive legs.

And second, well, that's the kind of solution that works best for knights like Ser Ondine here.

(Ondine sat straighter as everyone turned and noticed her.)

Notice her bright, shiny full plate armor? And you carry a shield, yes? When you go into the field?

(Ondine nodded, then spoke louder to the room in general. "Yes. I prefer a kite shield and broadsword. Though I'd've likely started that fight with spear and shield, to keep some distance from the ogre. Might even have thrown a javelin to start it, if I had one with me.")

Good, sensible solution for a more traditional form of knight than I am. But as you can all see, I don't favor plate armor.

(Deirdre actually posed, showing off her rather impressive form as much as her maroon leathers. Ondine shook her head at that. It came too close to openly flirting with the common folk. And Ondine didn't think the common folk present were all that much more comfortable with it than she was. Yes, there were small sounds of approval here and there, but probably a lot less than Deirdre was expecting.

As with most things, however, if this troubled Deirdre, Ondine could see no sign of it.)

The way I fight works best when I have room to maneuver. Room that would be denied me in those tunnels.

So, yes, I could've gained a small tactical advantage by drawing the ogre to me. But I would've lost the tactical advantage of greater maneuverability. A wash, at best, and a risk, at worst.

Instead, I waited. The ogre had been moving around the chamber some, while he talked to himself. And I wanted to wait until he came a little closer. Close enough that I could close and strike him ... oh, a good two or three times before he even knew I was there.

Might give me a chance to end this good and fast.

Again, though, even for me, things rarely work out *that* well.

No, the ogre was maybe one big step away from my charge when he stopped and looked up my direction.

Not *at* me, but down the tunnel.

"Ow cum. 'Oo."

His face darkened in anger.

"'Oo! Me sme'. Ow! Cum ow!"

Sad as I am to admit this, I'd been listening to enough of this ogre's pidgin Common Tongue that I had a reasonably good grasp of the way he spoke. Good enough to understand that what he'd just said — or tried to say — was, "You. I smell you. Out. Come out."

So, with a sigh and the complete loss of any chance for a nice, quick ambush, I stepped into the chamber.

"You are a thief," I said. "And a murderer. And a cannibal. And I am here to stop you from doing all three of those things."

"Canna..." the ogre tried to say, frowning.

"You ate a human."

The ogre actually nodded. Rubbed his belly and smiled. "Guh!"

I didn't want to understand what he meant by that, but I was sure he meant that the human tasted good. Which was not helping increase his life span.

I smiled at him. A nasty kind of smile. Rather like this one here.

(Deirdre smiled then, and everyone who saw it shuddered. Even Ondine.

Ondine had known or known *of* Deirdre for quite some time. Respected her. Had been amused by her and embarrassed for her and even occasionally shocked by things she'd done.

But it wasn't until that moment that Ondine actually *feared* Deirdre. Because that smile, it suggested that Deirdre wouldn't just carve her way through her enemies when she needed to.

That smile suggested that some part of her would enjoy it.

And that idea worried Ondine more than a little.

But then the quality of that smile changed, and the room relaxed. And Deirdre just looked like the playful reprobate Ondine had known. Which made her wonder. Was that evil smile a mask? A trick to frighten enemies?

Or was that playful smile the true mask?)

And as I gave him that smile, spread my weapon hands wide and said, "Well, there's another human right here. And I bet I'd taste a whole lot better than those nasty sheep. Come eat *me* if you can."

(Ondine half-expected a few suggestive comments or laughs at that line, but no. Either the crowd had been thrown by that smile, or they were enough in the moment that they were too focused on Deirdre's coming fight with the ogre for a sex joke.)

To my surprise, the ogre didn't charge. In fact, he moved to put the fire between us.

"Way," he said, which I didn't get until he held up a halting hand.

He wanted me to wait? He actually wanted to *talk*?

Then the bastard kicked a burning log at me. Sparks flew everywhere as a fiery log the size of my leg came flying at me arrow fast.

I dove to my right and rolled away.

The ogre had his club now. Swung it.

I kept rolling. The ground shook as his club head slammed into the rocky floor behind me.

The ogre roared. Frustrated, maybe, that he hadn't killed me yet. He tried to stomp me flat. Maybe trying to control my dives and rolls and leaps. To herd me where his club could get me.

I let him stomp a few times while I evaded him. Let him build a rhythm in his head, for how the fight would go.

Then I snapped out of a roll, and dove back the way I'd come. Straight between his legs. And before tucking into my roll, I cut him twice. My rapier slashing one calf, my dueling dagger the other.

I came to my feet and sprang at him as he turned to face me, club moving high.

Height worked against him there. Yeah, he could gain a lot of momentum with each swing, but that club had to travel a long way up before it came back down again. And even *his* huge muscles could make that happen only so fast.

So my spring let me sink both dagger and rapier into his left thigh.

Took his balance. He tipped. Staggered, while I came down to land beside that leg.

I leapt away a split second before that club came down so hard it snapped.

The ogre now held half its club in each hand. He wasn't standing steadily, but I didn't trust that. He'd proven crafty enough already.

So I danced back around to the other side of the fire. He might've been exaggerating how much he felt those cuts, but he was still bleeding from them. More from the stabs than the cuts, of course. Hide as thick as he had. Still. Viscous black blood that bubbled from his wounds and oozed down his legs.

And the more blood he bled, the weaker he'd get. Though big as he was, might be a while before he noticed.

"Ki' 'oo," he growled.

"Not if I kill you first."

He tried kicking another burning log at me. Not because he expected it to work, but because last time I'd dived to my right and he figured I would again.

I know this because I dove *left* this time while he stomped to the other side of the fire from me.

But now I stood near one of the supports for the spit, which still held all three of those big, stolen sheep.

Channeling a little extra power through my rapier, I slashed right through that support.

The sheep crashed into the fire. Dimming the light. Flinging sparks everywhere. Filling the air with smoke and the smells of burning wool and burning sheep.

"Foo'!" the ogre yelled, surging forward to save his meal.

I leapt somersaulting through the air to land on his back as he bent down to grab the spit.

I shoved my rapier upward through the back of his throat and into what passed for his brains. Straight to the hilt. Point coming out of the top of his skull.

As the blade went in, I stabbed his neck rapidly with my dueling dagger. Over and over and over. Deep as each thrust could go.

The ogre fell forward into the fire. More sparks. More smoke.

Hacking and coughing, eyes watering, I held my place on his back. Stabbing with that dagger until his neck wasn't much more than pulp.

I didn't trust that he was dead yet. Something as tough as an ogre, you can't count on it stopping just because you've done enough damage to kill something like, say, a dozen oxen. I fully expected this bastard to stand up again if I stopped stabbing.

So I didn't. I worked my rapier around inside his skull while my dagger did its work. And once I'd done all I could there, I pulled both blades out and went after where I expected his heart to be.

I only stopped once the ogre caught fire and didn't seem motivated to do anything about it.

Figured that meant it *might* be dead.

But best to be sure.

I gave the head three swift kicks, until it came free from that pulped neck and rolled down across the rocky ground.

*Now* I knew that thing had to be dead.

And let me tell you. In my not-so-humble opinion, the smell of a burning ogre is much more pleasant than the smell of a living ogre.

## 10

——————

FINALLY CONVINCED THAT *THIS* OGRE WAS DEAD, I LEAPT DOWN FROM MY perch atop the burning corpse to the safety of the rocky ground.

The air was thick with smoke, and the smells of burning sheep and ogre. Which clings to the tongue, let me tell you.

Didn't mean I was done though.

Yes, *this* ogre was dead. But I couldn't risk that there weren't others around here. Mommy and Daddy, perhaps.

So I checked around those tunnels for a while, just to make sure that it didn't have any company. Or worse, prisoners.

Never did find any of either, though.

Now at this point, I was exhausted. And my lungs were ready to rebel and install a new queen, if I didn't get them something like fresh air sometime soon.

Plus, there was no way I was going to sleep in this ogre-befouled place.

No, I had visions of this inn. This common room. The wonderful food and ale here. And those sweet, soft beds upstairs. All of that was dancing in my head. And if getting to those things meant marching back through the cold, dark night, well, then that was what I'd do. Even bone-tired as I was.

So I collected the ogre's head, as proof, and wrapped it in a couple of those mountain goat hides. And I took another of those hides with me back to that first chamber, where I gathered the remains of that dead human to bring back as well. For funerary rites.

Then, well, there's not much more to tell. I made my way back here — got back maybe by ... midday? — you people were good enough to feast me for three days, as thanks.

You were even kind enough to let me get some sleep first, so I could enjoy it. Which, let me tell you, I really appreciated.

Oh, by the way, how long did you keep that ogre's head on a spike?

("Two aetts," the bartender said. "Then it got too rancid. If you'd brought that head back during high summer, probably wouldn't have lasted three days.")

And I never did find out. Who was the dead man?

("A miner," the bartender said. "Not from our town, but from Fadellid, up the road. Lenner was his name. Word was he'd gotten lost trying to take a shortcut back from the mines.")

Well, I hope his remains gave his family and friends some peace.

And if you guys ever have trouble with another ogre, I think you know who to send for.

(The crowd burst into applause, and Ondine couldn't help joining in.)

# EPILOGUE

Once Deirdre jumped down from the table, the musicians started up again and the common room came to life around Ondine. Some folks singing, others talking, and all of them eating or drinking or both.

Ondine was a little surprised, though, that Deirdre came and sat beside her. That big farm boy had to move to make room for her, but he didn't seem to mind. In fact, he couldn't stop blushing.

"Didn't expect to see you *here* tonight, Ondine," Deirdre said, smiling. "What brings you out this way?"

"The mines."

"Ah." Deirdre's smile broadened. "The *right* number of knights for that job."

They both chuckled.

"So do you come out here every year to celebrate killing the ogre?"

Deirdre shook her head and wrinkled her nose. "No, I just had to get out of Water's End for a while."

"Don't tell me you've gotten on Duke Aefric's bad side. I had the impression you were one of his favorites. I mean, he named you *ducal champion*."

"Yes, he did," Deirdre said with a warm smile, as though the title had some kind of subtext Ondine wasn't aware of. "No. I haven't managed to upset his grace. Though I can't say the same for some of his advisers." She chuckled. "It's just that, well, after more than a solid aett of celebrating his grace's marriage, I thought it might be fun to come someplace that would celebrate *me* a little."

Ondine thought there was something more to it than that. Something in Deirdre's eyes...

Was she jealous of the duke's new wife? She couldn't have held aspirations that direction herself?

Could she?

No.

Impossible.

Deirdre didn't have the standing or holdings or even an important enough *name* to be considered a possible bride for his grace.

Not to mention that she caused enough trouble around the ducal court as things were. As the duchess consort...

"Well, as long as you're here," Ondine said, "want to come check on the mines with me? Be good to have someone to talk to on those long rides."

"How long will do you figure this will take?"

"Two aetts at the most. Unless there's trouble, and I don't have reason to expect any."

Ondine wasn't sure, but she thought she heard Deirdre mutter, "That ought to be long enough."

Louder, Deirdre said, with a smile, "Well, no one should be riding alone in weather like this anyway. I'll be happy to come along."

And so Ondine's mission didn't get any warmer. It even snowed before they were done. But at least she had companionship and laughter. And those things, they made a mission like this one much easier to bear. Even in the heart of winter.

# SIGN UP FOR STEFON'S NEWSLETTER

Stefon loves to keep in touch with his readers, and loves to keep you reading. The best way for him to do both is for you to sign up for his newsletter.

Sign up at http://www.stefonmears.com/join

If you sign up for Stefon's newsletter, you get...

- Monthly updates about his publishing and travel schedules
- His latest news, in brief, and answers to reader questions
- A free short story for signing up
- List-only offers and occasional specials
- Plus a free short story every month!

# ABOUT THE AUTHOR

Stefon Mears has heard some strange tales told in bars. Stefon has more than thirty novels to his credit, and he never stops writing. He earned his M.F.A. in Creative Writing from N.I.L.A., and his B.A. in Religious Studies (double emphasis in Ritual and Mythology) from U.C. Berkeley. He's a lifelong gamer and fantasy fan. Stefon lives in Portland, Oregon, with his wife and three cats.

*Look for Stefon online:*
www.stefonmears.com
himself@stefonmears.com